HEAVENLY HOSTS

Eucharistic Miracles for Kids

Kathryn Griffin Swegart OFS

Cover art by John Folley
www.johnfolley.com
Illustrations by Hannah West-Ireland
ISBN: 9781729408681
Second Edition
Formatting: Ellen Gable Hrkach

To my grandchildren

"I am the bread of life; he who comes to me shall not hunger, and he who believes in me shall not thirst." John 6:35

All these stories are based on Eucharistic miracles documented by the Church.

Table of Contents

Introduction 1

Miracle of Skete, Egypt—Third Century.......................3

Miracle of Lanciano, Italy ---Eighth Century..................7

Miracle of Rimini, Italy – 1227................................13

Miracle of Assisi, Italy – 1240.................................17

Miracle of Kranenburg, Germany – 1280......................23

Miracle of Krakow, Poland – 1345............................27

Miracle of Avignon, France – 1461...........................31

Miracle of LaRochelle, France – 1461.........................35

Miracle of Pibrac, France – 1587...............................41

Miracle of Tumaco, Colombia – 1906.........................47

Miracle of Fatima, Portugal – 1916............................51

Miracle of Buenos Aires, Argentina – 1994...................55

The Real Presence:

A Lesson from Saint Philip Neri – 1555......................61

Real Miracles in Real Places.....................................65

INTRODUCTION

Eucharistic Miracles: God Lifts the Veil

Miracles happen every day in the most common places. Take a walk on a late summer day. Look under the leaf of a milkweed pod. A small green pouch hangs from a tiny silk button. Be curious and look closer. It appears that an artist with a fine brush has painted a sparkling gold rim around the top. Here is the chrysalis of a Monarch butterfly. Nothing moves. It looks like nothing is happening but looks can be deceiving. Inside this pouch, a caterpillar dissolves into liquid. A chemical process turns this liquid into a Monarch butterfly. Even scientists call this change a biological miracle.

Every time we attend the Holy Sacrifice of the Mass, a miracle happens. The priest elevates the host and says, "Take this, all of you, and eat of it, for this is my Body, which will be given up for you." Like the chrysalis, a big change occurs. We can't see this change. We believe it because Jesus told us so at the Last Supper when he instituted the Eucharist. Our Catholic faith teaches us that at the moment of consecration, Jesus is present under the appearances of bread and wine. He is there Body and Blood, Soul and Divinity. He becomes our spiritual food. The Real Presence of Jesus in the Eucharist is a mystery of God's love, Eucharistic miracles do not prove this great mystery; they strengthen our faith. We believe in our hearts.

Jesus loves us and wants to be near us. That is why He comes to us at Mass. He looks different, not like that picture of Him on a holy card. He is hidden under a veil of bread and wine. Sometimes God lifts that veil. Sometimes Jesus shows that the bread is His flesh and the wine is His blood. More than a hundred times in Church history, Jesus gives us a peek behind the veil. Here are twelve of those miracles. Some people and animals are imaginary, but every miracle really did happen.

When you attend Mass, remember these stories. If you use your imagination, you can picture Him in the Host. After you receive Him at Holy Communion, be thankful that He is with you in this beautiful miracle of the Eucharist.

MIRACLE OF SKETE

Egypt - Third Century

Father Luke stood in solitude, contemplating the Sahara Desert. He lived in Scetis Valley in Egypt with other hermits; his home was a hut made of mud. It was a place of refuge from his father, a camel driver who tried to live the hard life of a nomad in the desert. Off he ran into the Sahara and joined these desert fathers praying and weaving baskets out of marsh reeds.

Wind picked up sand and blew it into his face. He shielded his eyes. *Oh Lord, you brought be to this desolate place. You stripped everything from me: my family and all my possessions. In this lonely place, I must abandon all things and give my heart to you. This I cannot do. My heart is made of stone. I am too proud.*

Now a camel caravan appeared on a rocky plateau. *That is good*, the priest thought. *Merchants will trade grain for my baskets.*

Camels will entertain me. It was a small caravan. Father Luke watched intently as they approached. Each camel had heavy packs, swaying under the weight. Their padded feet moved quietly onto monastery grounds.

"Welcome," Father Luke said.

One merchant glared at him. His name was Marcus. Father Luke remembered him from past encounters.

"Watch our camels while we look at your baskets," said Marcus. "Last time I traded, your baskets had weak bottoms. Camel milk fell through and spilled on my feet."

Father Luke turned away, towards the camel. Camels were familiar to him. His father assigned him to care for the calves. He taught them to stand and kneel on command. Many times, they refused. He remembered moments from childhood. Once a camel was on the ground, it was a battle to get it to stand.

"Get up," he'd command and pull on a rope. The camel looked placidly at him through long, curly eyelashes. Luke pushed and pulled in frustration. It was like trying to move a giant boulder. Often his father watched.

"The camel is stubborn, just like you," his father said.

A gruff voice snapped Luke back to the present moment.

"I will trade for six baskets," Marcus said, handing him two bags of grain. "I will trade more bags next time, if these baskets are strong."

"That is fair. These baskets are strong. I test them with rocks," Father Luke said.

"I do not trust you. I do not trust any hermit. I hear that you are cannibals," Marcus said.

"Cannibals? We do not eat any meat, certainly not human flesh," the priest said.

"You lie. You eat human flesh at your rituals. Ancient drawings are carved on catacomb walls. You eat the body of Jesus and drink His blood."

"You misunderstand. At Mass, we use bread and wine as Jesus commanded. We do it to remember the Last Supper. Bread and wine are symbols, nothing more," Father Luke said.

"Let us hope that is true. I do not trade with cannibals."

Angrily, Marcus yanked on his camel. Rocking from side to side, the camel plodded away. It came as a surprise to Father Luke that he was being watched. A man was standing nearby. His superior, Father Daniel, stood quietly, pulling on his gray beard.

"Father Daniel, I did not know you were there," Father Luke said.

"I heard what you said."

"Yes, I do test my baskets. Do not worry. They are strong."

"I do not speak of baskets. I speak about the breaking of bread at Mass. You are gravely mistaken. Jesus was clear. We eat of His flesh and drink of His Blood. This is clearly written in Holy Scripture."

Father Luke squeezed the bag of grain. He felt like throwing it on the ground. Like a camel, he could not change his own nature. He had to speak honestly, "Father Daniel, unless you show me evidence, I will not change my mind. This teaching is difficult. Who can accept it?"

"Well, Father Luke, now you quote scripture. Jesus said... 'for my flesh is true food and my blood is true drink.' His disciples argued among themselves. How can this be? Many disciples turned back and no longer followed Him."

"I do not turn away from Christ; I follow Him. I work hard and try to live a holy life."

Father Daniel smiled. "We will pray that God shows you the truth. "

Luke was glad to see night fall on this day. He entered his hut and made a bed out of marsh reeds. As he drifted off to sleep, doubts filled his mind like storm clouds. At times like this, Luke was glad he was a hermit. He did not talk to anyone for many days.

Finally, Sunday came. Today he must follow the rule and gather at worship. As he entered church, Father Daniel grabbed him by the arm.

"Come, sit up front. Your brother hermits have prayed for you. In His time, God answers our prayers," he said.

"He has forgotten about me, lost in the desert as I am," Father Luke said.

Mass began in the usual way with scripture and a homily. Father Luke was tired from lack of sleep and found it difficult to stay awake. Reverently, Father Daniel prepared the gifts of bread and wine. He said the words, "This is my Body. Do this in remembrance of me."

At these words, a pulsating light burst out of the Host and a vision appeared. It was a vision of the Holy Child, lying in straw, wrapped in white blankets. How peacefully He slept. Father Luke felt transported back to the stable in Bethlehem. The baby moved, and His eyes opened. Father Luke's heart trembled at the sight and now *his* eyes opened. He proclaimed, "Lord, I believe that the bread is your Body, and that your Blood is in the chalice."

The real doubting monk who witnessed a vision of Christ Child in the Host lived in the Sahara Desert more than 1700 years ago. Two other monks observed this supernatural event. Like a fossil preserved in stone, this Eucharistic miracle is found in ancient writings of the Desert Fathers.

MIRACLE OF LANCIANO
ITALY – EIGHTH CENTURY

Swiftly racing across a black sky, storm clouds descended over the village of Lanciano, unleashing heavy rain on the countryside. Antonio drew covers over his head and groaned. His little dog, Pepi, curled up next to him.

"I must assist at early Mass today with Father Georgio, the grumpiest man on earth."

Pepi rolled on his back and yawned. Antonio rubbed his soft fur. Pepi's mouth was drawn up in a smile.

"Such a mysterious dog. Why smile on this darkest of days?"

Pepi leaped out of bed and looked up with eager eyes.

"Nothing good will come of this day," Antonio grumbled.

Wrapped in a woolen coat, Antonio opened the door. Sheets of cold rain smacked him in the face. Gusts of wind scattered fallen leaves at his feet. They swirled like miniature tornadoes; doors banged, and branches snapped. Pepi danced on the muddy path leading to the church of Saint Longinus.

Arriving at the church, Antonio spoke to Pepi, "Stay here. No dogs allowed in church."

He unlatched the door. As he did, Pepi bolted inside.

"Pepi, come back. Do you want to get us both in trouble?"

Pepi did not listen. He was having too much fun running around the altar. A shuffling sound came from the monastery, home of monks in the order of Saint Basil. Father Georgio was coming. There was no time to waste. Antonio made his move, but he was too slow. To Pepi, this was a new game. With a yelp of glee, he eluded Antonio's grasp and scampered about. He bumped into a statue of Saint Longinus. The statue glared at him with marble eyes.

"What is the meaning of this?" Father Georgio yelled. His voice was dark and dreary, like the storm raging through Lanciano.

"I am sorry, Father. I tried to catch him, but he's too fast," Antonio said.

"Get that dog out of here. Let's get this over with," he snapped.

Antonio felt a stab of confusion. Let's get this over with? What did he mean? Disgusted, Father Georgio turned and went to the altar. Roughly, he dropped unconsecrated hosts on the paten. A wave of discouragement hit Antonio. He thought about those wafers.

Pepi trotted over, wagging his tail.

"Pepi, how is it possible the bread and wine become the Body and Blood of Jesus? My eyes are not fooled. It is impossible."

Antonio watched the monk. He passed in front of the tabernacle and did not genuflect.

"Yes, let's get this over with," Antonio said in a weary voice. He opened the door. Rain lashed the chapel. With his tail down, Pepi walked into the storm.

"Antonio, light these candles, lay out the altar cloths. We don't have all day," Father Georgio said. He pulled green vestments over his head. In flickering candle light, his black eyebrows pointed downward in sharp angles, giving a perpetual look of anger.

Antonio sighed. He wondered if anyone would brave this storm to attend Mass. As a heavy gust rattled shutters, the door creaked, and several parishioners came inside. Antonio lit a fat tallow candle behind the altar. It was a gesture he did every day, but today something was different. A mysterious presence lurked somewhere nearby. He stared up at a carved crucifix hanging on the wall. In his last agony, Jesus looked down at him. Thorns punctured his forehead; light flickered on his bony rib cage. On his side was the wound, pierced by a Roman guard. Antonio touched a nail in Jesus foot. I want to believe in you with all my heart.

"Antonio. It is time to process," Father Georgio said.

Antonio lifted the long-handled cross and led the way. As

they entered, a small congregation stood. Antonio sat down and watched as the priest quickly read from scripture and skipped the sermon. As consecration of the bread and wine neared, Antonio picked up gold bells. Father Georgio held the white wafer and prayed, "This is my body. Do this in remembrance of me." As he lifted the host, his hands began to tremble.

"My Lord and my God," he gasped.

Antonio leaped to his feet, "What is wrong, Father?"

Tears streamed down the monk's face and his shoulders shook, wracked by deep sobbing. Antonio looked at the gold plate. A white wafer was transformed into human flesh – a round disc of light pink skin. It reminded him of the time he fell on a sharp stick, pointy as a spear. It punctured his stomach, leaving a flap of skin above the wound.

Father Georgio stared in the chalice. "The wine, it is gone. Now there is blood, real human blood."

He looked up at the congregation.

"O good people, Our Lord has revealed Himself to our eyes! Behold the flesh and blood of our Most Beloved Christ."

An old man, stooped from years of labor in the fields, stood up and asked, "What has happened?"

"Come see. The Lord is really here on the altar," Father Georgio replied.

Gently, the farmer helped his wife to her feet. In hushed reverence, people followed and gathered near Father Georgio. As he showed the miraculous flesh, they all fell to their knees.

Antonio stared in wonderment at the scene before him. Joyful thoughts filled his mind. This must be how those shepherds felt on that first Christmas morning. Like them, he wanted to tell the world. Running up the steeple stairs two at a time, he pulled hard on the rope. Bells pealed out. Come and see this great miracle. Jesus Christ has come to earth. Rejoice!

THE MIRACLE OF RIMINI
ITALY - 1227

Juniper, the mule, plodded on under a blistering sun, his flanks shiny with sweat. A boy named Angelo pulled up on the harness.

"One more row to plow," he said. "Papa said we will plant a vineyard here and grow the most succulent grapes in all of Italy."

Angelo led Juniper to the cool shade of an olive tree. As always, a bale of hay awaited him. It was not a bad life for the old mule. He worked hard but was fed well in return.

Angelo pulled a cluster of grapes out of a basket. "On this hot day I have a special treat for you."

Juniper closed his eyes, savoring every drop of sweet juice.

How peaceful it was, mule and boy resting beneath an olive tree, not a care in the world. The quiet was broken by the sound of a man yelling angrily. Curiosity got the better of Angelo. He tied Juniper to a tree and meandered down to the village. Crowds gathered around two men who were in a debate about God. One of the men was Father Anthony of Padua, a Franciscan friar dressed in brown robes. He was a young priest, famous for his holiness.

The other man was Angelo's father, Bonovillo, who shouted, "If you, Anthony, produce a miracle and demonstrate to me that communion is truly the Body of Christ, I will renounce my heresy and immediately convert to the Catholic faith."

Angelo loved his father but prayed that he would not be so stubborn. In Bonovillo's mind, he was right, and the Church was wrong. Many villagers agreed.

Father Anthony stared at the people. He had strong, sharp features and a gentle expression. Unafraid, he raised his arms to silence the crowd.

He spoke in a loud voice, "Have you forgotten the Lord's miracle performed here on your river banks? Since men refused to listen to the words of our Lord, I called upon fishes of the sea and river to hear His word."

Angelo knew of this miracle. Father Anthony summoned God's fish and they came to hear Father Anthony. In a most orderly fashion, they swam into neat lines and turned to him. This multitude of fish opened their mouths in praise of God.

"Such a child's tale you expect us to believe?" Bonovillo asked.

Now this stirred the crowd to near frenzy and they chanted, "Bonovillo! Bonovillo!"

Egged on by the crowd, Bonovillo strode towards Father

Anthony until they were nose to nose.

"Let's make a bet. I'll keep one of my beasts locked up for three days to feel the torments of hunger. Then I'll bring it forth in public and show it food. You will stand in front of the beast with the Host. If the animal, leaving aside the food, hurries to adore the Host, I will share the faith of your Church."

Dizziness swept over Angelo. He knew what animal his father would use. It did not seem fair that Juniper should be punished for his father's stubborn heart. Angelo tried to explain the bet to Juniper. As the hours passed, the mule gazed mournfully at hay stacked in a stall. Day one of the bet ended. Juniper's empty stomach growled him to sleep.

Day two was not much better. A hungry mule is an angry mule. He kicked the stall in dismay. Angelo brought him buckets of water. Juniper lapped it up eagerly, but it did not fill his stomach.

On day three, Angelo stayed all day in the barn, being careful not to eat in front of him. Juniper trembled from starvation.

On day four, Bonovillo burst into the barn, "Angelo, load the wagon with hay. Look what I have brought – delicious grapes."

Juniper wanted to leap over the stall to eat the grapes. Alas, he was too old for that feat. Instead, they led him to the village where Father Anthony awaited them. In his hands he held a monstrance containing the Blessed Sacrament. A throng gathered in the village square.

Bonovillo dangled the grapes in front of Juniper's nose. The mule sniffed the cluster of purple fruit. He hesitated. To the wonder of all, the animal did not eat.

Bonovillo yanked on his reins, "Come on, Junipcr. You

love grapes. I have a big basket of them. Don't be a fool. Eat!"

He shoved Juniper's head into the basket.

"Papa, he does not want to eat. Leave him alone," Angelo said.

"Of course, he wants to eat," Bonovillo said. He spit on the ground. Bonovillo always spit when he was angry.

Juniper snorted in Bonovillo's face, then ambled towards the monstrance. The old mule had pains in his knee; Angelo knew this for a fact. *Kneeling is impossible,* Angelo thought. On this day, pain did not matter to Juniper. Father Anthony held up the monstrance and prayed, "I bless you brother mule, in the name of the Father and of the Son, and of the Holy Spirit. Amen."

Before all the villagers, Juniper knelt in front of the Blessed Sacrament. Angelo wondered what his father would do. He had many faults, Angelo knew that, but Papa was a man of his word. Bonovillo fell to his knees next to the old mule.

"May God forgive me for all my sins," Bonovillo said.

From that day forward, Bonovillo proclaimed the Real Presence to all his neighbors. Every day he visited Juniper in the barn. The old mule twitched his big ears happily when Bonovillo opened the barn door. He knew a succulent cluster of plump grapes was coming his way.

MIRACLE OF ASSISI

ITALY - 1240

Gatta, the cat, sat on her haunches and watched nuns cutting bread for the noon meal. As they bustled around the kitchen, their brown robes swished like gentle breezes. Gatta pricked her ears in hope that a morsel would fall her way.

"You are an old cat, but your hearing is sharp as a kitten, "Sister Maria said as she brushed a pile of crumbs onto the floor.

"Yes, she hears trouble, like mice scratching in our cupboards," said Sister Anna.

Gatta lapped the floor clean and ambled away.

"Every day it is the same. Gatta visits the kitchen for a crust of bread and then stays with Sister Clare," Sister Maria said.

"Gatta brings comfort to Sister Clare in this terrible illness. The doctor said she will never walk again," Sister Anna sighed.

As Gatta plodded through the convent, her paws clicked on the shiny wooden floors. She stayed alert in hopes of hearing mice squeaking. She arrived at Sister Clare's bedroom and pushed the door open with her nose. Sister Clare smiled and patted her bed.

"Your spot is warm. Brother sun shines brightly through the window. Our Lord takes care of his creatures."

Gatta climbed onto Sister Clare's bed and snuggled next to her frail body. Gently, Sister Clare stroked her soft fur. The old cat purred. Within minutes, they both were fast asleep. In this cozy warmth, Gatta often slept deep into the afternoon, but not today. She heard a small noise. Gatta lifted her head abruptly and listened. It was the sound of men whispering. She clawed urgently at Sister Clare's arm.

Slowly, Sister Clare opened her eyes.

"What is wrong, dear Gatta? Did you eat spoiled cheese?"

Gatta stood bolt upright. Fur bristled down her spine. She jumped off the bed and bounded to the window sill. Her yellow eyes stared intently at high stone walls surrounding the convent. She heard the grunt of a man heaving a heavy object in the air. A grappling hook clattered against the stone and clamped onto the top of the wall. Attached to the hook was a thick rope that buzzed with tension as an invader pulled it tightly. Once again, she heard a hook whiz through the air and catch the top of the wall. Within minutes, a row of hooks lined the wall. The air was filled with the sound of boots scraping the wall. One after the other, heads appeared at the top. Each man wore a black mask with holes cut for eyes, nose, and mouth.

Gatta growled deeply, like a lioness protesting her cubs.

Sister Clare heard the battle cry of Saracen warriors. Instantly, invaders swarmed over the walls, trampling vegetable gardens and knocking down fences. Armed with arrows and axes, they raced to the convent doors.

Feebly, Sister Clare raised herself up on her elbows and cried out, "My sisters, we are under attack! Bolt the doors and windows! Someone bring me the Holy Eucharist! May God protect us."

As the alarm went out among the nuns, they wept and screamed for help. With a thunderous crash, the Saracens struck the doors with battering rams. The old wooden doors began to crack and splinter. Only a few more blows and the doors would shatter, letting in masked invaders breathing murderous threats. Bam! The main door began to split.

Fifty terrified nuns clustered around Sister Clare's bed, weeping with anguish. Gatta maintained her watch at the window. Sister Maria rushed in carrying a silver box containing the consecrated Host. She pushed her way through the crowd.

Sister Clare's eyes fell on the precious box. "It is the Body of Christ. He will protect us. Place it on a stand by the front door. "

Sister Maria and Sister Anna grasped her under the arms; they carefully lifted Sister Clare out of bed and carried her towards the front door.

Outside the door, the commander let out a blood-thirsty cry, "One more thrust and we will be inside the convent. By the time we finish with them, they'll wish they'd never been born."

Sister Clare laid flat upon the ground and prayed loudly, "Lord save us from these evil men. I cannot do this myself." Gatta weaved her way through the cluster of nuns and stood at Sister Clare's feet. Sister Clare seemed to listen to an inner voice.

"I hear you, Lord. You will always defend us."

For a moment, there was silence as the commander examined the door. His fingers passed over the rotting timbers and loose hinges. He rubbed his forehead in confusion. Five of his strongest men ran at the door, barreling into it like a cannonball. Still, it did not break. He leaned forward and listened. A woman's confident voice came through the cracks.

"Behold, my Lord, is it possible that You wish to deliver these defenseless handmaids into the hands of pagans? I pray, Lord, protect these handmaids."

She held up the silver box. All the nuns saw bright lights shine from the monstrance.

Outside, the commander stepped back, feeling threatened by an unseen power.

"Sir, do you wish us to run at the door? One more thrust should break it down," his assistant said.

In battle, the commander often called on Allah to bring death to his enemies. Now a weak woman called on her God for protection. A powerful force dwelt behind the battered door, a force greater than Allah. To break through that door, to murder these women, could bring down the wrath of their god. His shoulders slumped in resignation.

Turning, he snapped out orders. "Back over the wall. Leave these women to their poverty."

Instantly, the troops scrambled over the wall and disappeared.

Silence reigned inside the convent. Sister Maria handed Sister Clare the silver box. She hugged it tightly and said, "My Lord and my God."

Gatta spotted crumbs on the kitchen floor. Her stomach

growled, but she did not move. She snuggled next to Sister Clare. Her wet nose touched the silver box. Peace flowed through her body, warmer than the afternoon sun flooding through the window.

THE MIRACLE OF KRANENBURG GERMANY - 1280

Karl and Franz leaned their shepherd sticks at the chapel door. Karl did not want to enter for Holy Mass. He always had an excuse for not going. Somedays it was too cold. Somedays it was too hot. Today he was hungry for the sausage and bread in his leather sack. Karl watched his friend bless himself reverently before entering the chapel. *If only I could be close to God, just like Franz, I would be happy,* he thought, but he brushed aside the thought.

"Let's skip Mass today. I am not even awake," Karl said sleepily.

"It is Lent. We must prepare our souls for Easter," Franz said.

Karl tried another tactic. "I feel sick to my stomach."

"You'll survive," Franz said, giving him a nudge.

The old pastor, Father Joseph, shuffled out of the sacristy. He was a holy priest, but Karl tried to avoid him for confession. Some people thought Father Joseph could see into your heart.

"Look at the crucifix my son," Father Joseph often said. "You nailed Jesus to the cross by your sins. You pierced His side with your lukewarm faith."

This could not be true. Karl did not consider himself lukewarm. Let's just say he was easily distracted and much too busy tending sheep to bother with prayers. Let old ladies with rosaries do the praying.

All of this thinking so early in the morning made him restless. At Holy Communion, Karl kept the Host in his mouth, but didn't swallow. Concealing this fact from Franz, he left church immediately and went out into a garden.

Heavy rain began to fall; Karl sought shelter under an oak tree. He leaned against the rough bark and tried to swallow the Host, but it stuck in his throat. As the chapel door opened, Karl turned his back. He spit the Host into his hand and threw it against the tree. He turned toward Franz and pretended everything was fine.

Franz patted him on the back, "You look pale. What is the problem?"

Nothing more than throwing a Host on the ground, Karl thought, *nothing more than mortal sin.* He looked at the kind face of his friend and realized he could trust Franz.

"Well…I couldn't swallow the Host…so I…spit it out."

Franz furrowed his brow, "Let's look for it."

"It should be right here, by this big root."

"I don't see it," Franz said.

Karl searched frantically at the exact spot where the Host had fallen. "It seems to have disappeared into thin air."

"We have a mystery on our hands. I believe that we will get the answer, but not now. Someday you will learn about the strange disappearance of the Host," Franz predicted.

They crawled in the wet grass, carefully feeling around the root. They turned over every stone; filtering through clumps of grass proved fruitless. So immersed were they in the search that they did not see Father Joseph watching them.

"Did you lose something?" he asked.

Karl looked up into the face of the priest. Father Joseph wore a black hat pulled down over his face to keep out the rain. Water dripped off the broad brim. Slowly, Karl stood up, trying to think of what to say. Father Joseph waited patiently. He wore glasses with thick lenses that seemed to magnify his eyes. Once again, Karl felt Father Joseph could see right through him. Karl looked down at his muddy boots and couldn't speak.

"Let's go back into the church and have a talk," Father said.

As spring changed to summer, Karl often thought about the strange disappearance of the Host. It should have been there, right under the tree.

Two years later, Karl heard that men were cutting the oak tree down for firewood. He decided to look for the Host one last time. Perhaps it was buried deep in the soil, underneath a root. When he arrived, woodsmen were already there, chopping at the massive trunk. They were strong men and experts in the art of cutting trees. Karl knew one of them. His name was Eric; he had been cutting trees for many years. Their sharp axes gleamed in the sun, chopping at the hard wood. Like the rhythm of a clock, they alternated strokes, cutting through a hundred years of growth. Finally, they were close.

"Timber!" they cried.

The oak tree fell with a loud thud.

"Okay, it's safe," Eric said.

It was all a routine matter until they examined the tree more closely. Eric took off his cap and scratched his head. He said, "Now I've seen everything!"

Karl moved in for a closer look. He saw a small crucifix carved from the wood of the tree. Mysteriously, it was imbedded in the trunk. A master craftsman created Christ at the moment of death. Karl gazed upon the crown of thorns, the cruel nails, and His pierced side. Had the Host turned into a crucifix? The mystery perplexed him but excited all the villagers. News of the miraculous crucifix spread far and wide.

Never could Karl have imagined that hundreds of years later, the crucifix still exists. A Gothic church was built in honor of the miracle. To this day, pilgrims stand to marvel at the wondrous cross, created from the sin of a repentant shepherd.

MIRACLE OF KRAKOW

POLAND - 1345

Under cover of night, two thieves crept up to All Saints Church. It was Stanley's idea to break into the church to steal the gold cup. Joseph had misgivings. Stealing kept food on his table, but stealing from the Church?

"Give me the crowbar," Stanley whispered.

Joseph dug into his bag and handed him the tool. There was no turning back.

Stanley pried open the door and went inside. All was black except for a red lamp burning next to the tabernacle. Joseph knew what the red light meant. It made him more nervous, but Stanley forged ahead. He popped open the tabernacle door, grabbed the cup containing consecrated Hosts, and ran into the woods.

The next day they examined their booty. Stanley held the cup to the morning sun.

"This is not real gold," Stanley said with disgust.

"So, what should we do with it?" Joseph asked.

"Dump it somewhere. Anywhere," Stanley said.

Joseph felt darkness overcome his mind, the darkness of a guilty conscience. He decided to act quickly and then forget about the whole messy affair. Joseph threw the cup into a nearby swamp and ran away. The cup tipped over and consecrated Hosts spilled onto the mud.

Jesus in the Hosts did not like sitting in the muck. He had to let people know He was there. The Hosts began to blink, just like fireflies on a summer evening.

It happened that a boy named Stephen and his dog Honor walked to this swamp every day to throw away trash.

"I'll be glad to get rid of this stinking pail of garbage," Stephen said to his dog.

Usually, Honor went into the swamp to forage for scraps. Not today. He stopped dead in his tracks and sniffed the air.

"What's wrong, Honor?" Stephen asked.

Usually the swamp was a dismal sight, all brown and gray. From behind a pile of garbage, small white lights blinked.

"There must be ghosts in there," Stephen said.

Just as noon bells tolled at All Saints Church, he ran to spread the news. Farmers stopped plowing, children stopped playing, and mothers stopped cooking. It was time to say the Angelus. A blistering sun scorched the countryside. On days such as this, the villagers gathered under the shade of a sycamore tree.

As the faithful finished their prayers, Stephen and Honor

ran up to the tree.

"Lights are blinking in the swamp! Miraculous lights!" he shouted.

The parish priest, Father Bernard, stood in the midst of the crowd.

"God has made a strange day for us," Father Bernard said. "First the Hosts are stolen and now mysterious lights. Let us go to the swamp.

Honor bounded ahead, down to the swamp. Panting from the heat, he sat and waited. Father Bernard leaned heavily on his walking stick as he led the faithful.

"Father, look! The lights! They are even brighter than before!" Stephen exclaimed.

Struck with fear, the good people stopped walking. Over the marsh grass and black stumps of dead trees, a starburst of white crystals lit the sky.

Father Bernard knew when the Holy Spirit was at work. He believed there was a connection between the lights and the missing Hosts.

"We must tell the bishop," he said.

The entire village marched to the bishop's house and Father Bernard knocked on the door. At the sight of the crowd, Bishop Andrew knew something important had happened. He listened patiently to Father Bernard as he told the peculiar story.

"…I do believe the missing Hosts are in the swamp. God, forgive those thieves," the priest concluded.

"We cannot know that for sure. We will fast and pray for three days. If we still see flashes over the swamp, we will investigate," said Bishop Andrew.

With each passing day, the flashes grew brighter and Stephen grew hungrier. He watched Honor lap up a bowl of corn mush. Fasting would be so easy if Stephen didn't feel starved all the time.

On the third day, the entire village followed Bishop Andrew and Father Bernard to the swamp. Bishop Andrew lifted up his robe and waded ahead. Rays shone from one spot. Bishop Andrew looked down and saw Hosts, still perfectly clean, glowing like the sun. Carefully, he placed each Host back in the cup. After he climbed out of the swamp, Bishop Andrew held the cup high over his head. Awestruck villagers fell to their knees, crying and praying.

Stephen hugged Honor in wonder that God chose a humble boy and his dog to discover such a wondrous miracle.

MIRACLE OF AVIGNON
FRANCE - 1433

Driving rain beat on Brother Thomas as he sloshed through deep mud, slowly making his way towards the barn. He was a brother in the order of Gray Penitents and his work was to care for farm animals. Day after day of gloomy weather had settled in his heart. Soaked to the bone, Brother Thomas opened the barn door. Sebastian, their gentle work horse, whinnied softly.

Brother Thomas pulled an apple from his pocket. "It has been raining for seven days, my friend. We should build an ark."

As Sebastian crunched on the apple, Thomas said, "All this rain has ruined our crops. I don't know what we will eat. God has forgotten us."

Every day, Brother Thomas shared his deepest thoughts with Sebastian, who nuzzled Thomas and never talked back.

It was safe to tell Sebastian his darkest secret.

"My mind is troubled. I have come to doubt that Jesus is truly present in the Host. Perhaps I should run away and become a stable boy."

Sebastian twitched his ears with annoyance. Rain lashed the barn. Brother Thomas listened to rushing waters from the Rodano River, now at flood levels.

Just then, he heard men shouting. His superior, Father Armand, appeared at the door; water dripped off his cowl.

He yelled over the howling winds, "Brother Thomas, row me to the chapel. The Blessed Sacrament is on the altar. We must rescue It. The chapel is in danger of flooding!"

"But, Father, I am not a strong man. Choose another," Brother Thomas said.

Now this was a lie. The truth was that he did not want to risk his life saving a wafer of bread. Father Armand suspected these doubts preyed on Brother Thomas. It was obvious to anyone with eyes to see. Brother Thomas spent more time in the barn than on his knees praying. Father Armand also knew that God had a plan regarding this young man.

"No, you must be the one to row me to the chapel. Quickly, there is no time to waste," Father Armand said.

Sebastian backed up and looked away. It was horse talk that said, "You can't hide behind me anymore."

Since he found no support from Sebastian, Thomas pulled up his cowl and left with Father Armand. At the river, they hauled a heavy wooden boat into swirling currents. Brother Thomas gripped the oars and fought to keep them from capsizing in the rapids. Within minutes they were at a bend in the river.

Father Armand pointed to starboard, "Row over there."

As they pulled to shore, gravel scraped the boat bottom. They climbed out and ran through a pasture of wet grass. Arriving at the chapel, they looked back in horror. The river bank overflowed, and a mass of churning water rushed towards them.

"God, save us!" Father Armand cried out.

River water crashed into the desperate monks, knocking them down. Brother Thomas thrashed in the torrent, struggling to stand up. He wiped water from his eyes and saw wild, tumbling foam thunder towards the altar. A gold monstrance sat on the altar. Inside the glass window was the Host, like a white eye, staring out at them. Suddenly, a mighty wind swept through the chapel, sucking up the flood into towering walls of water, one wall on each side of the middle aisle. Miraculously, a clear path led straight to the Blessed Sacrament.

Timidly, Father Armand put one foot on the stone floor.

"Follow me," he said.

Brother Thomas felt like his feet were stuck in wet mud. He pictured tons of water crashing down on his head.

Father Armand spoke gently, "Jesus will protect you. Trust in Him."

Brother Thomas took a deep breath. "One step at a time."

Slowly, they crept down the aisle, staring at a wondrous sight. Like two giant waves, walls of water towered over them in sheets of marbled foam. As they approached the altar, the rain stopped. Father Armand and Brother Thomas fell to their knees. Sun burst through a stained-glass window and light sparkled off a gold crucifix that adorned the monstrance.

A great miracle occurred that day, but none greater than a change in the heart of one humble Gray Penitent.

MIRACLE OF LAROCHELLE
FRANCE - 1461

Few people would look at the graceful apple tree and believe that a terrible accident happened there. It grew behind the house where Bertrand and his family lived. Tall, with spreading limbs, ruby red apples hung from every branch. Bertrand and his younger brother Vincent craned their necks to find the best climbing route.

"I will go straight up the trunk and inch my way out that branch in the middle, then drop apples down to you," Bertrand said.

"That is very high. Mama and Papa would say it is too dangerous," Vincent warned.

"They worry too much. Besides, they have not seen me climb. I am graceful as a monkey," he said.

With that Bertrand grabbed hold of a limb and swung upwards. Pausing, he surveyed a thick branch laden with burgundy apples. It was higher than his original plan, but worth the risk.

He pointed, "I am going after those apples. They are beauties."

"Don't do it," Vincent yelled, but it was too late.

Bertrand climbed higher and shimmied onto the limb. He reached for the apple and heard a crack. Almost in slow motion, the branch shook beneath him, and broke. For a second, he felt suspended in mid-air and tried to grab onto something but missed. Branches and blue sky swirled in his vision. Helpless, Bertrand fell like a stone and crashed in a twisted way on his neck. He lay deathly still. Vincent thought for sure that his brother was dead. Vincent ran into the house to get his parents. Shocked by the sight of his limp body, they prayed desperately to God that their son would live. With tender care, they carried him into the house.

Many days passed before Bertrand opened his eyes. At first his vision was blurry. Shadowy figures moved about the room, talking in hushed tones.

"Bertrand. It is Mama. Where does it hurt?" she asked.

He tried to move his tongue.

"Can you talk?" she asked.

He said nothing.

"Can you move your arms?"

His arms were heavy as boulders.

"Can you move your hands, your legs?" Panic rose in her voice.

Bertrand felt trapped in his own body, paralyzed from the neck down. For weeks, he tried to talk, but words froze in his mouth. Although his heart was strong, and he could swallow, Bertrand refused to eat. To live in this prison was worse than death.

Mama and Vincent would have none of that attitude.

"Vincent, run and get Father Jacques," Mama said.

Vincent ran quickly to find Father Jacques. He was in the rectory preparing lunch. At the sight of the frightened boy, the priest grabbed the bag he used for bringing sacraments to the sick and followed Vincent back home.

Bertrand opened his eyes at the sound of the priest's voice.

"I bless you with these holy oils. Trust in the Lord and His great mercy," Father Jacques said.

Gently, he blessed Bertrand with holy oils. The fresh balsam smell of the oil awakened something in him. Closing his eyes, Bertrand imagined walking through a pine forest, breathing in deeply, fully alive. Hope stirred anew. *Maybe someday I will walk again*, he thought.

Miracles of a different sort occurred every day over the next five years. Papa built a bed so Bertrand could sit up and look out the window. Mama put seeds on the window sill to attract birds. A small gray bird visited every day, cocking his head and chirping, "Cheer up. Cheer up." Vincent played by the bedside, making soldiers out of sticks and forts out of sheets. Bertrand could not talk or move, but Vincent often said," I see your eyes smiling."

In spring of the fifth year since Bertrand's terrible accident,

Vincent returned from Sunday Mass and spoke with great excitement.

"Father Jacques said I am ready to receive First Holy Communion. This Easter will be very special."

A deep desire for Holy Communion welled up inside of Bertrand. He grunted loudly.

"What did you say?" Vincent asked.

Bertrand tried to unlock his tangled tongue but failed.

"Me, too! Is that what you said?"

Vincent looked into his brother's eyes.

"You are smiling. I will go ask Father Jacques."

On that Easter morning, Father Jacques walked solemnly toward Bertrand's house. He had a Host tucked safely in his pocket. As he entered Bertrand's house, Father Jacques whispered a prayer. Bertrand looked ready. His hair was combed, and he was dressed in a white suit. Father Jacques held up the Host.

"Do you believe this is Jesus, the true Lamb of God?"

Bertrand looked at Vincent.

"His eyes say yes," Vincent said.

Father Jacques leaned over and placed the Host on Bertrand's tongue. Instantly, Bertrand felt a surge of energy flow through him. Like sunshine melting a frozen river, his limbs broke free from the paralysis. For the first time in five years, he wiggled his feet, shook his arms, and raised himself off the bed.

A most happy scene erupted in that bedroom. It was a moment of tears and hugs and great rejoicing. Bertrand walked over to the window and looked at the sun as it shed warm rays upon the earth. After five silent years, he spoke his first words, “Our help is in the name of the Lord.”

If someday you travel to LaRochelle, stop into the cathedral. There you will find a painted manuscript with a picture of Bertrand dancing for joy.

MIRACLE OF PIBRAC
FRANCE - 1587

One day a little girl dressed in rags crawled to the open window of a house. Her name was Germaine, and in all her eight years no one loved her because she was thought to be ugly. She had a paralyzed arm and her dirty hair was tangled in knots. Germaine looked in the window and saw her stepmother, Hortense, baking gingerbread. That spicy smell tickled Germaine's nostrils and made her smile. *If only I could have a tiny morsel,* she said quietly. Hortense had sharp hearing and whirled around, stomping to the open window.

She shouted, "Get away, you horrid worm of a girl, or I will beat you with a broom!"

Germaine responded in a gentle voice, "Might I have a scrap of apple core from the garbage heap?"

"Those are for the pigs. Now get to the barn with the animals where you belong," Hortense said and whacked the child with her broom.

That was not the first time Hortense had beaten Germaine. In fact, Germaine had many yellow and black bruises on her thin body. As she headed to the barn, she watched the sun set in bright orange rays. Her tender soul felt the warmth of God's love, and she prayed. *Dear Lord, forgive the cruelty of my stepmother for she knows not what she does. I pray that one day she may enter heaven and be at peace.*

Germaine's home was a big barn, filled with the smell of hay and horse manure. Clover, the kindest cow in the world (or so Germaine believed) licked the child's bleeding brow. Sheep stood in a circle around a pile of hay, waiting for Germaine to snuggle up in her hay bed and go to sleep. Animals were her only friends in the world. How peaceful it was in the barn, listening to the breathing of horses and the soft bleating of lambs. Outside the barn, neighborhood children taunted her with rhymes like "Stinky, stinky just like Pinky. Pinky, Pinky the smelly old pig." In the village, mothers walked in wide circles around her, afraid their own darling children would catch some icky germ.

Every day, Germaine went out to watch the family's flock of sheep. Hungry wolves stared out from the forest that bordered the pasture, but they never attacked Germaine or the flock. Every day the church bells rang, calling the faithful to daily Mass. As you may have guessed, Germaine was devoted to Jesus and His presence in the Blessed Sacrament. Every day she propped her shepherd's staff in a pile of rocks, asked her guardian angel to watch over the sheep, and headed off to church. Without fail, the sheep were protected from prowling wolves. Villagers began to notice her holiness and stories began to circulate.

One winter's day, a neighbor saw Hortense beating Germaine, for her stepmother believed that Germaine had stolen bread and was hiding it in her cloak. It was a frightful sight for the neighbor to see, but then a miracle occurred. Crusts of bread did not tumble out of her coat. Instead, brilliant flowers, like never before seen in all of France, fell to their feet. Germaine handed Hortense a flower and said, "This flower is from God. He wants to forgive you." From that day on, even the hard heart of Hortense began to soften. She invited Germaine to stay in the house, but Germaine preferred to sleep in the barn.

News of this event spread throughout the village.

"I don't believe these fairy tales," stated a know-it-all seamstress named Muriel. She decided to spy on this supposedly holy child, watching as the child walked to daily Mass. Muriel hid in bushes near a river brimming over with spring rains and melting snow. Foam boiled in a torrent of white water. *She will never get across today or she will drown*, Muriel said to herself. *She will not risk her life just to eat a paltry white wafer at Mass.*

Germaine stopped at the edge of this rushing stream. She prayed aloud, *Jesus, You know that I want to receive Holy Communion. If it be Your will, bring me safely to church.* Jesus heard this prayer, as He always does. Not only did the waters slow down, but the torrent ceased moving altogether. Muriel's eyes really popped when she saw the river part into a dry path, perfect for Germaine to pass through with not even one drop of water on her feet. Now Muriel was slightly on the plump side and not accustomed to running, but run she did, through thickets and over rocks, eager to spread news of Germaine's miracle.

Villagers began to act in a peculiar fashion. Suddenly, Germaine was invited to meals morning, noon, and night. She sat at long wooden tables and marveled at bowls of delicious food. For the first time, she tasted roasted chicken, hot biscuits with gravy, and green beans picked fresh from the garden. One night, Muriel invited her over to share in a big pot of vegetable soup. As Germaine sipped her first spoonful, there was a knock at the door. There stood Hortense holding a pan of warm gingerbread. Hortense looked humbly at the floor and said sweetly, "I baked this for you, Germaine. It is fresh out of the oven." Such a happy meal it was for all to savor. Muriel ladled soup for Hortense who graciously said, "thank you." Germaine took a bite of the gingerbread and announced, "This tastes better than I could ever imagine."

Villagers prayed that Germaine would grow strong and healthy. Sad to say, Germaine's bones and skin and heart were worn out from years of neglect. One winter's night, she settled into her bed of hay, content to feel the warm breath of sheep; they huddled closer to her. Meanwhile, out in the forest, two monks tried to find their way home in the black night. Suddenly, the night was illuminated by a burst of dazzling brightness. Beams of light streamed through the sky and down on the rooftop of an old barn-Germaine's barn. They rubbed their eyes in disbelief. Celestial beings moved inside the bright stream, on a mission to bring some holy person to their heavenly home. That was the guess of the monks, and that guess was correct.

As the first rays of dawn awakened God's creation, the sheep bleated, but Germaine did not tend them, as she had done every day for many years. Hortense heard the sheep and went out to the barn. She found the frail body of Germaine, lying dead in the hay, but with an angelic glow on her face.

How glorious was her funeral! Muriel wove a garland of flowers to put on Germaine's head. Hortense bought her a new dress, fit for a princess, and in the girl's hands she placed a white candle.

In 1867, Pope Pius IX canonized Germaine. On June 13th, Catholics around the world celebrate the feast day of this humble saint, a child that turned over her sufferings for the conversion of sinners.

MIRACLE OF TUMACO COLUMBIA – 1906

Crystal blue waters of the Pacific Ocean lapped at Maria's feet as she looked for shells. Her little sister, Anita, piled mud into a sand castle.

"Don't cry when the tide washes it away," Maria said.

"Anita doesn't cry anymore. I'm a big girl now," Anita said.

"A little wave knocks you down and you cry. Anita is not a big girl yet," Maria said.

"Don't say that," Anita began to cry.

"Here is a shell for the top of your castle," Maria placed a pink scallop shell in Anita's hand. She smiled and stuck the shell on top.

Maria dug her feet into the sand. As she did, the beach trembled slightly under her feet. It was a faint tickle, but she knew what it meant. From the time she could first understand, Mama warned her, "If you feel the earth begin to shake, run as fast as you can. A tsunami is coming."

Tsunami. Maria knew tsunami. An earthquake underneath the ocean creates giant waves that wipe out entire towns. Maria picked up Anita and ran.

"Why are we running?" Anita asked. Maria held tightly to her sister.

"A big wave is coming. We must run," Maria said.

"Where are we going?"

"To a safe place."

Anita did not ask any more questions. In her fear, she squeezed Maria's neck. Maria was glad Anita was quiet because she did not know where to go. As she ran through an open market, Maria saw merchants selling fruits and vegetables. Little boys played tag amidst the food carts. Women chose colorful bouquets of flowers for their kitchen table. They did not know that a tsunami was coming.

A church bell rang out over the village. It rang ten times. Exactly at ten o'clock, the earthquake struck. The ground shook violently for ten minutes. Maria heard a loud bang as the earth split under her feet. People screamed; babies cried. Anita held on tightly to her big sister.

One man yelled out, "Run to the church. Father Gerard will help us."

Like a flock of frightened sheep, they all ran to the Church of Santa Domingo. Father Gerard met them at the door. In his hand, he held a monstrance containing the Blessed Sacrament.

"Let us go, my children. Let us all go toward the beach, and may God have mercy on us," he said.

Maria wanted to shout at the priest. *This is wrong. We don't walk towards a tsunami. We run away,* she thought. So many words tumbled in her head. *No, Father Gerard, do not lead us to death. We are too young to die.* She hugged Anita and wept. Caught in the middle of the frantic throng, Maria could not escape.

"He is taking us the wrong way," Anita sobbed.

Maria forced herself to say, "We must trust him. We must trust that Jesus will protect us."

Holding the monstrance high over his head, Father Gerard led the procession. Approaching the beach, surf pounded the shore in a symphony of booms. Maria held her breath and listened. Now she heard a sucking sound and grinding as currents dragged stones over the sand.

Now like one organism, the people gasped. One mile out to sea, an immense tide moved rapidly toward them, swelling into a train of waves. It grew by the second. A wall of water sixty feet high raced towards them. Closer and closer it came. Maria craned her neck to see the monstrous height.

Father Gerard turned towards the faithful. "Do not be afraid. Jesus is with us."

Bravely, the priest moved towards the wave. He raised the monstrance and made a sign of the cross over the ocean. In defiance, the monster roared towards the beach. This was Maria's last second of life. She closed her eyes. Strangely, she thought of Anita and not herself. *Anita did not deserve to die. She will never build another sandcastle.*

She braced for the tidal wave to break and heard the people cry, "Miracle! Miracle!"

Maria opened her eyes. Little Anita pointed in wonder.

Tsunami froze in one spot, like an invisible hand was at work. Wispy white clouds reflected in the shimmering blue surface. In this moment of salvation, tsunami retreated, away from land, and back into a crystal sea.

MIRACLE OF FATIMA
PORTUGAL – 1916

One spring day, Francisco ran to the pasture, carrying a burlap bag. In this pasture, Francisco knew he would find snakes. He knew how to capture them: lay flat in the tall grass and wait patiently. As he did, a fat brown snake slithered his way. Francisco grabbed him by the tail and stuffed the squirming reptile into his bag, pleased to bring him home to show Mama and his younger sister Jacinta. Rain began to fall, but drizzle would not stop him from capturing more lizards. He was eight years old and filled with curiosity to see what adventures awaited him. On the crest of a hill he saw sheep grazing. They were watched by his older cousin Lucia and Jacinta.

"Francisco, you wandered off again! I can't keep this flock *and* you together. Your sister obeys me, and you must too." Lucia scolded.

That was true, Jacinta was obedient, but she was only six and afraid that wolves roamed the fields. Francisco was older and not afraid of wolves. Still, Mama said to listen to his 10-year-old cousin and that was what he must do. As he released the snake back into the pasture, steady rain began to fall.

"Let's take shelter in that cave," Lucia said. It was a small cave carved into the side of a hill, but for Francisco, he imagined it a den of wild animals, a place where he could wrestle lions and bears and emerge triumphant. As rain poured down on the fields, Francisco heard another sound. Wind swept in a startling burst, shaking an olive tree in the field. Francisco crawled out of the cave to look overhead for black clouds. Instead, he saw a white light over an olive tree, brighter than any full moon. Shaped like a crystal ball, it moved over the field and toward the cave. At first, Francisco thought it was a dream, but no, this shining light was not a dream, but real. A young man in flowing robes stood inside the light.

"Fear not," he said. "I am the Angel of Peace. Pray with me."

Caught in this mystical moment, swept away from everyday life, all three children fell to their knees and listened to the angel say a prayer three times,

My God, I believe in Thee! I adore Thee! I hope in Thee, and I love thee! I ask pardon for those who do not believe, do not adore, do not hope, and do not love Thee.

The mysterious figure gazed down at them and spoke again. "Pray thus so that the Hearts of Jesus and Mary will hear your petitions." Like mist burned away by the sun, he disappeared, leaving the children in stunned silence.

When they went home, none of the children revealed these strange events to their families. Francisco felt his whole heart burn with fiery love for the angel. From that moment on, life would never be the same for the children. Francisco grew more serious. Often, Mama felt his forehead for fever and looked down his throat for redness. Surely, he must be sick. Every day she declared him healthy and sent him off to tend the sheep with Lucia and Jacinta.

"Do you think the angel will come again?" Francisco asked Lucia, who could only shrug. One summer's day, the answer came. With a rush of wind and blinding light, the angel came again.

To Francisco, it seemed the angel spoke more loudly and in a stern voice. *What are you doing? Pray! Pray a great deal. The Hearts of Jesus and Mary have merciful designs on you. Offer prayers and sacrifices continually to the Most High. Make of everything you can a sacrifice and offer it as a sacrifice to God as a petition for the conversion of sinners. I am the Guardian Angel of Portugal. Above all, accept and bear with submission the suffering which the Lord will send you.*

Once again, the angel vanished in the blink of an eye, leaving the children deeply saddened by his message. Francisco could not help wondering if the angel made a mistake. After all, he liked to play just like other boys, and sometimes he even got into trouble. Lucia even told him he prayed the rosary wrong to make it go faster. Somewhere, there must be another child that was more deserving of a celestial visitor. Still, he prayed harder and offered small sacrifices. He tried not to think about suffering, for that put fear in his heart.

Weeks passed, and the nights grew colder. Fall arrived, and with it, came the Guardian Angel of Portugal, this time bringing gifts. In one hand, he held a shimmering gold chalice; in the other hand, he held a Host. Drops of blood fell from the Host into the chalice. He seemed to place the chalice and Host in invisible hands that hovered in the air. The angel lay flat on the ground, worshipping the Body and Blood of Jesus. Three times he said this prayer:

Most Holy Trinity-Father, Son, and Holy Ghost-I adore Thee profoundly. I offer Thee the Most Precious Body, Blood, Soul and Divinity of Jesus Christ, present in all the tabernacles of the world, in reparation for the outrages, sacrileges and indifference by which He is offended. And through the infinite merits of His Most Sacred Heart, and the Immaculate Heart of Mary, I beg of Thee the conversion of sinners.

Francisco fell to his knees, trying to say the prayer. Now the Angel of Peace moved toward the children. In this sublime moment of grace, they all received the Precious Body and Blood of Jesus Christ.

All that you have just read really happened to the children of Fatima. Perhaps you know what occurred the following year. The Blessed Virgin Mary appeared to the children six times. In October of 1917, a spectacular miracle occurred before an immense crowd of 70,000 people. As reported in newspapers throughout the world, the sun spun and danced in the sky.

These apparitions, including visits by the Angel of Peace, have been fully investigated and approved by the Church. Fatima has become a major pilgrimage site visited by millions of people every year.

In 2017, Francisco and Jacinta were canonized by Pope Francis, declaring this little boy who liked to capture snakes, a full-fledged saint in the Roman Catholic Church.

MIRACLE OF BUENOS AIRES
ARGENTINA - 1994

As they walked towards a pond, it was evident that two children were on a mission. They carried wide-mouthed jars and wore rubber boots. They dipped jars into the water and held them up to the sunlight.

"We caught one," Rosie Ortiz said to her younger brother Pedro.

Pedro studied a tiny insect swimming in their jar.

"He swims very fast. What is his name?" Pedro asked.

"This is Daphnia, a most complex species of water flea," Rosie said. "He should work very well for our study."

"But I just want to play in the mud," Pedro said, jumping in the water. Spray splashed onto Rosie's glasses.

"Later. We have something to prove to Papa," Rosie said, wiping her lenses.

"You can not prove anything to Papa. He knows everything. He is the smartest man in the world. He is a famous doctor," Pedro said proudly.

"That is true, but there is one thing I must prove to him."

Pedro squished his boots in the mud, half-listening, "What is that?"

"Papa does not believe in God. I will prove it to him. He gave me a microscope for my birthday. I will find my proof."

Back in their bedroom, Rosie used a pipette to drop Daphnia onto a life slide. An indentation in the glass slide kept the bug from swimming away. She turned a focusing wheel.

"There he is. Every part of him is moving. Cilia, like hundreds of tiny wings, beat rapidly near his mouth. Pedro look here," Rosie said.

Pedro looked through the microscope. "Unbelievable! You can see right through him."

Rosie studied her specimen again.

"I see food passing through his stomach and blood flowing." Rosie sharpened the focus. "I can even see his heart beating. How can anything this complex happen by accident? Intelligent design-that is what we have here."

"I agree with you, but there is one thing you are forgetting," Pedro said.

"And what is that?"

"Papa is very stubborn. It will take more than a water flea

to convince him. We need a miracle."

"Perhaps you are correct, but I will submit my study to him," Rosie bent over her desk and began drawing.

That evening, Rosie stood outside Papa's office. His door was shut. Papa spoke loudly to someone on the telephone. Rosie put her ear to the door. She picked up most of the conversation. Cardinal Bergoglio, archbishop of Buenos Aires, was on the telephone.

"Yes, Cardinal. How can I help you?"

Dr. Ortiz listened.

"You say a consecrated Host turned into human flesh?" Dr. Ortiz asked.

For several minutes, Dr. Ortiz listened carefully to the Cardinal's words.

"Most Reverend Cardinal Bergoglio, let me see if I have the story correct. After Mass, a consecrated Host was found on the rim of a candle holder. A woman brought it to the priest, Father Perez. Since it was too dirty to eat, he put it in a cup of water and placed it in the tabernacle, hoping it would dissolve. One week later, Father Perez opened the tabernacle. To his amazement, the Host turned into an enlarged piece of bloody flesh. That is when the priest called you. What did you do?"

Dr. Ortiz was silent.

"You had a professional photographer take pictures of it, put it back in the tabernacle, and kept it a secret. How long was it a secret?"

The doctor paused.

"Three years. Father Perez opened the tabernacle. The flesh still floated in distilled water and did not dissolve." Dr. Ortiz cleared his throat. "Most Reverend Cardinal, I beg to differ.

Over time, flesh dissolves in water."

More listening.

"This is a very interesting story. How can I help you?"

Rosie pressed her ear harder on the door.

"You want a scientific study? Very well, I know just the man: Dr. Frederic Zugiba, from New York. He is one of the world's foremost cardiologists and forensic pathologists."

Cardinal Bergoglio spoke on his end.

"I agree, Cardinal. We will not tell Dr. Zugiba where it came from. My secretary will call and set up an appointment for me to take a sample from this…what did you call it?"

Pause.

"Eucharistic miracle."

Dr. Ortiz hung up the phone. Rosie hesitated. This did not seem like a good time to show her father proof for the existence of God. She took paper out of her pocket. There Daphnia was in all its glory-eye, antenna, brain, heart, and swimming feet. He was one perfect swimming, eating machine. Rosie knocked.

"Come in," Dr. Ortiz said, sounding irritated.

Rosie decided to smile in hopes Papa would smile back. He did.

"Well, it is good to see you. To what do I owe the pleasure of your company?"

"I have something for you," Rosie said and handed him the drawing.

Her father studied it. "Well done. I will put it on my bulletin board."

Rosie continued. "It is more than just a drawing Papa. Look

on the back."

Dr. Ortiz flipped over the paper and scowled.

"So, you think the complexity of a flea proves God's existence? Daphnia is purely the result of natural selection occurring over thousands of years. It is survival of the fittest."

"But, Papa…"

"Do not join the ranks of fools who believe in fairytales. Cardinal Bergoglio is an intelligent man, but he believes a wafer turned into human flesh. Unbelievable! I will prove it is a hoax. I am very tired. Good night."

Dr. Ortiz did not sleep well that night. This whole business of Eucharistic miracles troubled him. He tossed and turned. With great pleasure, he would give the results of Dr. Zugiba's study to the cardinal. The report will distress him, but that happens to honest people when faced with facts

It took weeks. Finally, an official looking envelope arrived, special delivery. Dr Ortiz hurried into his office. He tore open the top and began to read:

"I have definitively determined that this sample is a fragment of a human heart. There were many white blood cells. This means the heart was alive when the sample was taken. White blood cells die without a living organism. In addition, the white blood cells penetrated the tissue. Therefore, the heart was under severe stress as if the owner was severely beaten.

Severely beaten, Dr. Ortiz collapsed in his chair and squeezed his eyes shut. He thought of Michelangelo's *Pieta*, a marble statue. Mary, the mother of Jesus, holds her dead son. She looks down at Him with intense sorrow.

"This cannot be true," he said.

He studied Dr. Zugiba's report. "But it is."

Dr. Ortiz leaned back in his chair, deep in thought, so deep that he lost track of time. His thoughts were interrupted by another knock at the door.

"Come in."

It was Rosie, holding her drawing of an insect. *This surely is the proof*, she thought. "Papa, I know you don't believe in miracles or God, but please look at my drawing."

He put on his reading glasses. "Let me take a closer look."

Several minutes passed before he looked up at Rose and smiled. "This is very convincing. I will give this matter further consideration."

Excitement crept into her voice. "Further consideration…that means that maybe one day you will believe! I must tell Pedro!"

She ran down the hall chanting in her head, *further consideration…further consideration.*

Indeed Dr. Ortiz did give the matter further consideration. The doctor had a change of heart so great that he traveled the world telling the story of Argentina's Eucharistic miracle.

THE REAL PRESENCE
A LESSON
FROM ST. PHILIP NERI - 1555

Snow fell lightly on rooftops in the Italian village. As Bertha sat on hard pews at church, complaints sprouted up like weeds. Instead of prayers, she muttered to herself.

"My legs hurt. I cannot kneel."

"My back hurts. I cannot stand."

"My head aches. I cannot pray."

She looked up at the altar and came up with a plan to leave early.

Father Philip Neri elevated the Host and say the words of consecration. An altar boy rang little gold bells. The tingling sound was a signal. That white wafer was no longer a white wafer; it was the Body and Blood, Soul and Divinity of Christ under the appearance of bread. Father Neri raised the chalice and said the words of consecration. Again, bells rang out softly, declaring the sacred miracle. Wine no longer existed. It was the Blood of Christ under the appearance of wine.

Bertha couldn't be bothered with the bells and what they meant. Her plan was in place. Receive communion and sneak out the back door. Beat the crowd home to a nice warm fire. Besides, she had to take care of…Bertha rubbed her forehead in worry. Anyway, no one will notice. Receiving the Host, she scooted out the door.

One thing didn't work out as Bertha planned. Father Neri saw her leave the church.

"Roberto and Paul, come here," he whispered to the two altar boys. "See the lady leaving the church?"

"The one with a gray shawl?" Roberto asked.

"Yes. Light two candles and follow her for several minutes."

"But why, Father?"

"She received Communion and then left without praying. The Real Presence of Jesus in the Eucharist dwells in her. That woman is a living tabernacle until the Host is digested. Perhaps she ignores Christ within her. Perhaps she has good reason to leave. We can only guess. You must go. It is a way to adore Our Lord and keep her company. Now go quickly."

They grabbed their coats and lit two candles. They pushed through the heavy front doors. Bertha walked briskly ahead of them.

"We better trot or she'll be out of sight," Paul said.

They protected the candles under their coats and caught up to Bertha.

"Excuse us, lady," Roberto said.

Bertha turned and scowled. "Don't bother me. Can't you see I'm in a hurry?"

Roberto opened his coat and held up the candle. "Father Neri sent us to walk with you."

"I don't need company. Now, go," she snapped.

"He said you just received Communion. He said you are a living tabernacle until the Host is digested. We have come to accompany you and Jesus," Roberto said.

"That is the most ridiculous thing I have ever heard. Get lost," she said.

Bertha turned down a stony path to her cottage. Roberto and Paul followed. She waved in disgust and slammed the door in their faces.

"What do we do now?" Paul asked.

"We should stand here a little longer until we are sure the Host is digested. Let's pray for her," Roberto said.

"I'm not praying for her. She's mean," Paul said, blowing out his candle. "Besides, it is hard to believe that a wafer is Jesus. It looks like a piece of bread."

Roberto looked at the sun rising over the hills. It tinged the slopes with golden light.

"Looks can be deceiving. For thousands of years, man believed that the sun traveled around the earth. Now we know earth travels around the sun."

"Maybe so, but I'm still not praying for her."

"You must. Jesus said to pray for our enemies."

At that moment, the door flung open, and Bertha stuck out her head.

"Get off my property or I will call the police," she shouted.

Roberto blew out his candle. He, too, was eager to leave this unpleasant woman. They walked slowly down the path Roberto looked back over his shoulder. He saw Bertha helping a crippled man walk on crutches. Gently, she helped him into a chair. Bertha poured hot tea out of a kettle and into a cup. The man's head drooped. With tenderness, she lifted up his chin and spooned tea into his mouth.

Roberto pointed in the window. "Paul, now look at the mean old woman."

Paul craned his neck for a better look. "I don't believe what I'm seeing."

As the sun rose higher in the sky, they started back to the village. On the road back, neither of them talked. They were too busy thinking many deep thoughts.

Real Miracles in Real Places

St. Francis Church - Lanciano, Italy

Temple of the Most Holy Eucharist - Rimini, Italy

St. Anthony of Padua and the mule

Convent of St. Damiano, Italy where St. Clare lived

Church of Saints Peter and Paul - Kranenburg, Germany

Church of Corpus Christi - Krakow, Poland

Chapel of the Gray Penitents - Avignon, France

Ancienne gravure du miracle d'Avignon

Engraving that shows the Miracle of Avignon, France

Home of St. Germaine - Pibrac, France

LaRochelle, France

Spot where Our Lady appeared, Fatima, Portugal

Children of Fatima

If you enjoyed *Heavenly Hosts,* you will love *Miraculous! Catholic Mysteries for Kids.*

Young readers can read about some of the most inspiring miracles in Catholic history. From the Miracle of the Sun to the Shroud of Turin, these engaging stories are sure to inspire everyone in your family. Illustrated. Ages 8 and up.

Brave Hearts

A Series Featuring Catholic Heroes and Heroines

Perilous Days: A Story of Faith and Courage

When a Nazi soldier knocks on the door of a quiet, Catholic family, life is thrown into turmoil. Teenage son Felix becomes an unwilling soldier in the German army. The family also must protect their young son Willy, who has Down Syndrome, from Hitler's extermination plan.

In a struggle to survive, Felix relies on his faithful dog and a mysterious stranger who hides shocking secrets. Historical fiction for ages 10-14. Recipient of the Catholic Writer's Guild Seal of Approval.

Martyrs

Father Sebastian Rale was a Jesuit missionary who lived among the Abenaki people from 1689-1724. In this riveting story, readers travel into the Maine wilderness and witness the courage of a true martyr for the Faith. Martyrs is an unforgettable story of courage, faith and enduring friendship.

Historical fiction for ages 10-14. Recipient of the Catholic Writer's Guild Seal of Approval.

Learn more about these inspiring Catholic books for young people at kathrynswegart.com

About the Author

Born in Boston, Kathryn Griffin Swegart earned a Master's degree from Boston College. She and her husband raised three children on a small farm in Maine. Kathryn is a professed member of the Secular Franciscans and author of *Perilous Days: A Story of Faith and Courage* and *Martyrs.*

Visit her website for more inspiring stories.

kathrynswegart.com

Made in the USA
Las Vegas, NV
27 May 2021